THE IMMORTAL COMBAT

Innocent Franklin

Amazon

I DEDICATED THIS BOOK TO GOD FOR HIS GOODNESS AND MERCIES. AND TO MY BELOVED BROTHER, AND MY LOVELY WIFE

CONTENTS

CHAPTER 1

Are You Born Again?

Passage: John 3:3-8
Focus: v16
"Except a man be born again, he cannot see the kingdom of God"

This is one of the most important questions anyone can be asked. You hear people say, are you a born again Christian? Is he born again? It is not enough to reply "I have been baptized (water baptism), and I go to church, and I supposed I am." Or to say: I have been born again from the womb.

If you claim to be born again, then, it should not stop at the point of confessing Jesus as your Lord and Saviour but you must go further to produce some fruits because by their fruits we shall know them:

Whosoever is born of God doth not commit sin and whosoever is born of God sinneth not (1 John 3:9, 5:18): That is, a man born again, or regenerated, does not commit sin as a habit. Sin no longer pleases him. Sin has become the abominable thing. We don't have to tell the person this is not good, he will know himself.

Whosoever believeth that Jesus Christ is born of God (1 John 5:1): a man born again, or regenerated believed that Jesus Christ is the only Saviour by whom he was pardoned. That He is a Divine Person appointed by God the Father for this very purpose and besides him there is no Saviour at all. Such person believes that for the sake of Christ's finished work and death upon the cross He is reckoned righteous in God's sight. He is convinced that Jesus is the Son of God.

And lastly, the man born again, or regenerate, is a righteous man. He wants and endeavours to live according to God's will, to do things that please God. His aim and desire is to love God with heart and soul, and mind and strength, and to love his neighbours as Himself. Such person always wants to be like Jesus, his heart will seek Christ every day of his life.
Now can you boldly say you are born again?

May the communion of the Holy Spirit be with you.

CHAPTER 2

Gang Rape

1 Corinthians 2:12-16 Focus: James 3:17 (KJV)

"But the wisdom that is from above is first pure, then peaceable, gentle, and easy to be entreated, full of mercy and good fruits, without partiality, and without hypocrisy."

I hope you have been enjoying the series on rape for this week. Gang Rape is when the rapists are more than one but two and above. In this case, the victim may not have the strength to really defend herself. The most important thing to do at this point is to pray.

How to pray in situation like this?
1. *You don't pray aloud:* At this point, you don't need to pray aloud for the rapists to know you are praying you may complicate the issue.

2. *You don't pray for the rapists:* You don't have to pray for the rapists in the form of begging them; they have made

up their minds before coming to you so begging them by praying for them will not matter.

3. *Pray in your mind:* The best and the only thing you can do at this junction is to pray to God in your heart (mind). He will hear you. He is the same God that hears Jonah from the belly of the fish.

Note that gang rape is more avoided than defended. Take heed to run away from all the causes of rape and take to heart how to escape from rape very well. Also, in the face of a gang rape, while you pray, God will provide a room of escape for you. Look out for it and take it immediately.

If raped; if there is a situation of rape either gang rape or otherwise, report to the appropriate authorities and people that could help you without delay especially health personnel. You need help physically, emotionally, psychologically and medically. You need to know what to do to prevent pregnancy resulting from such incident. You can see and talk to your spiritual or biological parents. You don't have to come to the outside world like a wounded person but as a stronger person. Also, a rape victim must remain chaste. You may not give account for that which has happened without your knowledge but you will surely account for all that will happen thereafter. And in case you need help, you can contact the source of this devotional.

May the communion of the Holy Spirit be with you.

1 Corinthians 2:12-16 [NLT]*

12 And we have received God's Spirit (not the world's spirit), so we can know the wonderful things God has freely given us.

13 When we tell you these things, we do not use words that come from human wisdom. Instead, we speak words given to us by the Spirit, using the Spirit's words to explain spiritual truths.

14 But people who aren't spiritual can't receive these truths from God's Spirit. It all sounds foolish to them and they can't understand it, for only those who are spiritual can understand what the Spirit means.

15 Those who are spiritual can evaluate all things, but they themselves cannot be evaluated by others.

16 For, "Who can know the lord's thoughts? Who knows enough to teach him?" But we understand these things, for we have the mind of Christ.

CHAPTER 3

Causes of Rape

Passage: **Psalms 1:1-6**
Focus: **Psalms 1:1 (KJV)**
Blessed is the man that walketh not in the counsel of the ungodly, nor standeth in the way of sinners, nor sitteth in the seat of the scornful."

The wicked act of rape is now rampant in our society as there are increasing cases of rape victims daily. Therefore, there is an urgent need for the cankerworm to be adequately addressed before it eats so deep to utter destruction. As much as we can never excuse a rapist, we cannot shy away from the fact that there are some things that lead to rape. Avoiding them will go a long way to shield a person from being a rape victim. The following are some of the causes of rape:

1. Dating (Boyfriend & Girlfriend relationship):
Many are in a romantic relationship with the opposite sex where they do different sexual activities like romance, kissing, cuddling, fondling, etc. but they don't want real sex. So, when the other party gets aroused and force their

way in, they claim that they were raped. Dating is an unguarded relationship where anything can happen. If you truly desire to be chaste, you will wait till you get mature and go into a godly courtship which alone is right before God.

2. **Lust:** This is a strong sexual feeling and/or thoughts you have towards another person. When you nurture lust, it could lead to rape.

3. **Bad Company:** Bad friends can pollute you to become a rapist or become a rape victim. Many ladies have been set up by their friends. Do not walk with children of the world or even someone that has a friend that is of the world. Walk with children of God. "Do not be misled: Bad company corrupts good character" 1 Corinthians 15:33 (NIV)

4. **Indecent Dressing:** Dressing to reveal the sensitive parts of your body (breasts, thighs, armpits, underwear etc) or too much tight fitting clothes could make you a victim of rape. If this can be stopped, the spirit of rape in the rapists will be dis-empowered.

5. **Lies:** A lot of people lie about the rape stories they tell. There was a lady that had made up her mind to lie to her husband in future that she was raped because she got into pre-marital sex with someone else, thinking that would make her go Scot free and avoid issues but it doesn't work that way. When you are not ready to tell lies, you will keep yourself by all means.

May the Communion of the Holy Spirit be with

Psalms 1:1–6 [NLT]

1 Oh, the joys of those who do not follow the advice of the wicked, or stand around with sinners, or join in with mockers.

2 But they delight in the law of the Lord, meditating on it day and night.

3 They are like trees planted along the riverbank, bearing fruit each season. Their leaves never wither, and they prosper in all they do.

4 But not the wicked! They are like worthless chaff, scattered by the wind.

5 They will be condemned at the time of judgment. Sinners will have no place among the godly.

6 For the Lord watches over the path of the godly, but the path of the wicked leads to destruction.

CHAPTER 4

How to Escape Rape

Passage: Proverbs 4:5-10
Focus: Proverbs 16:16 KJV;

How much better is it to get wisdom than gold! and to get understanding rather to be chosen than silver!

Having examined the causes of rape, it is very important to know how you can successfully escape being a rape victim. These are:

1. **Have a good mindset:** One very important idea you must have in mind is that NO SINGLE MAN CAN RAPE A SINGLE LADY WITHOUT HER CONSENT OR SURRENDERING. It is very important to treat a man that is about to rape you as if he wants to kill you, treat your virginity as very precious. You have power over rape to a larger extent so you have to be empowered with that mindset. The man trying to rape a lady is far weaker than the lady. The same thing for a lady who wants to rape a man.

2. **Be Time Conscious:** Do not travel late at night so you don't fall into the hands of opportunist. Plan your day so well and walk in broad daylight. If you must walk at night, hold bright light and walk with someone or walk faster. Also walk with your senses active, immediately you notice any strange movements around you, run as far as your legs could carry you.

3. **Report:** Once anyone is making any sexual advancement towards you, no matter who they are; even if they are your parents. Report to a trusted and trustworthy person. Don't keep shut. A closed mouth is a closed destiny.

4. **Boldness:** Do not exercise fear in the face of rape. Once you are overwhelmed with fear, the rapist gets more boldness to do his evil works.

5. **Be ready to defend:** Use all your power and strength to defend yourself just as you will struggle to defend if someone wants to kill you

Tomorrow, I will tell you what NOT to do when you are face to face with a rapist.

May the communion of the Holy Spirit be with you.

I will treat myself as a precious treasure and guard myself accordingly.
I Declare financial provisions and surplus to you all my readers in Jesus name Mark 11:24
READ 1 Chronicles 13-15, 2 Timothy 2

CHAPTER 5

Passage: **Mathew 8:1-4**
Focus: **v3**
_*And, Jesus put forth his hand, and touched him saying, I will; be thou clean. And immediately his leprosy was cleansed.

Matthew 8:1-4[NLT]*

1   Large crowds followed Jesus as he came down the mountainside.

2 Suddenly, a man with leprosy approached him and knelt before him. "Lord," the man said, "if you are willing, you can heal me and make me clean."

3 Jesus reached out and touched him. "I am willing," he said. "Be healed!" And instantly the leprosy disappeared.

4 Then Jesus said to him, "Don't tell anyone about this. Instead, go to the priest and let him examine you. Take along the offering required in the law of Moses for those who have been healed of leprosy. This will be a public testimony that you have been cleansed."

Healing is one of the specialties of the ministry of Jesus on earth. It is even part of his purpose on earth, Luke 4:18he hath sent me to heal the brokenhearted... he healed all who asked him and it has always been in an instant, if you can believe you can receive your healing now! Matthew 8 is my favorite healing passage of the scripture, because it exposes healing cases Jesus settled on a go and we shall be exploring the chapter in terms of healing.

I want you to know that Jesus is the healer, ready, willing to heal you whenever and wherever you call on him. Have you ever wondered why the gifts of healing and of working of miracles were given? Christ knew such a weapon will be important for believers to stand against bodily sicknesses and diseases, and to stay healthy to bring his kingdom come on earth as it is in heaven.

Take away the mindset that God made you sick to teach you a lesson or because you sin. Though sin has its own consequences, but God will never do that, there is no evil in him and sickness is evil. He is merciful and compassionate, He is always with us anytime we are lonely, devastated and psychologically down. We are the ones that must discover Him like what the leper did and come to the throne of grace to seek mercy in our time of need.

Much more than that Christ being willing to heal you is that, he has paid for your healing once and for all on the cross, the only process left is for you to claim your healing. Oh! Only if you understand that he has power over all bodily diseases, why we haven't experienced healing is because we no longer have faith or trust in the Christ. Those who ask by faith will never go back empty handed.

May the Communion of the Holy Spirit be with you! Amen

Claim your healing now and you can do so on behalf of

your friend and family!

I Declare that the light of God should shine bright in your life

When a man approached Jesus among the midst of the group

He if you are willing, you can heal me and make me whole

I believe if he truly know what Jesus is capable of doing, he would have been straight in his saying

But Jesus saw his brave move and responded I AM WILLING and healed him

Jesus from the beginning is a healer I've never for once come across a place in the scripture were Jesus was not able to heal any illness

Even at a point where His disciples couldn't heal a particular sickness. He took over and sickness and healed it

What am i trying to say, Jesus is the only answer to any sickness

He's a healer, a deliverer and a burden lifter.

Healing already part of Jesus even before He's ministry on earth

He's that one man that, even you don't ask Him heal you, he will detect it himself and heal you

He sees, He feels, and He solves

Like he said, cast all your anxieties on him

I don't know what is that your problem

Have you tried all mean?

And it didn't work?

I want you to try Jesus.

Remember the woman with the issue of blood for a solid twelve years....

She has spent all he had before she had an encounter with Jesus

After good twelve years of trying

Men and brethren, in every of our dealings, let's remember Jesus first.
He is one of the healing specialists. According to the book of Luke 4:18

He also heals the broken hearted according to the
And lets not forget, He doesn't disappoint, He is doesn't fails, and doesn't postpone His promises
Just make your request known unto Him and relax your mind for results.
I believe God will help us in Jesus name Amen I don't know what you are passing through or suffering from, but by the power of Jesus, i command your healing to take place now in Jesus name!
Thank you Jesus.
May the communion of the Holy Spirit be with you all

CHAPTER 6

Immortal Combat

Text: **Luke 14:28-32**
Focus: **v31**
"Or what king, going to make war against another king, sitteth not down first, and consulteth whether he be able with ten thousand to meet him that cometh against him with twenty thousand?"

Luke 14:28-32 [NLT]

28 "But don't begin until you count the cost. For who would begin construction of a building without first calculating the cost to see if there is enough money to finish it?

29 Otherwise, you might complete only the foundation before running out of money, and then everyone would laugh at you.

30 They would say, 'There's the person who started that building and couldn't afford to finish it!'

31 "Or what king would go to war against another king without first sitting down with his counselors to discuss whether his army of 10,000 could defeat the 20,000 soldiers marching against him?

32 And if he can't, he will send a delegation to discuss terms of peace while the enemy is still far away.

I told my people about the existence of and the current position of the devil, so whether you are kind, easy going, peaceful, not a trouble maker, etc. let me announce to you again that the devil is wicked and cunning and he has been cast down to the earth. Moreover, he came with great wrath. It is a common saying that we are in the midst of spiritual warfare, which goes on day and night. Many times, Christians have been told to fight demons, witches and wizards without proper preparation, forgetting that a standard battle doesn't begin on the battlefield.

The military counsel:
Jesus, who is the Army General of heaven gives us the most basic military counsel in our focus. You must first sit to count the number of soldiers in your own army and then count the number of soldiers in the army of your opponent. Jesus went further to say; After counting, you strategize: "Can I make my own 10,000 to defeat their 20,000?" In counting, you look for strengths and weaknesses, the advantages and disadvantages of your own army, compared to his and then re-strategize.

It is like a football match. The coach of a team must first look into his own team, identify his key players and their fitness then consider the footballers of the other team and then strategize. How come Christians are only told to FIGHT and FIGHT and we aren't told to first count our own army?! We don't look at our strengths and weaknesses, our advantages and disadvantages, as well as that of the opposing soldiers. We aren't even taught the strategy!

The following are things to have to build a formidable

army:

Add to your faith virtue, to virtue add knowledge, to knowledge add self-control, to self-control add perseverance, to perseverance add godliness, to godliness add brotherly kindness, and to brotherly kindness add love. Our enemy is immortal and we were once under his domain and numbered as his army but at Salvation, we were converted into the LORD'S ARMY. We will not win this battle if we still walk in the flesh, which is the old man. Have you ever wondered why after you prayed and fasted over a particular matter, it leaves you for a while but after some days or months you are back to it? The enemy has not given up on you and you must die daily to flesh. Your army is not yet formidable.

May the Communion of the Holy Spirit be with you.

I am from this day forward, a formidable army.
Is our words from now on. Bind every spirit of discord, frustration and strife that might seem to be growing among group members and leaders.
2 Chronicles 9-10, Hebrews 7.

There is much need for us to sit down and estimate a cost something before going to get it
Understanding the fact that without making a sound research about a topic or theme
You can't get a clear picture of it
Bible reading
Focus is its   verse 31
"Or what king, going to make war against another king, sitteth not down first, and consulteth whether he be able with ten thousand to meet him that cometh against him with twenty thousand?"*_

The Lord bless his word in our heart in Jesus name amen
Before going or rushing in marriage there is a need for us to it down, study, analysis, estimate, get nourished, get everything planned before you start it
so whether you are kind, easy going, peaceful, not a trouble maker, etc.
It is a common saying that we are in the midst of spiritual warfare, which goes on day and night.
Moreover, he came with great wrath.
let me announce to you again that the devil is wicked and cunning and he has been cast down to the earth.
Many times, Christians have been told to fight demons, witches and wizards without proper preparation, forgetting that a standard battle doesn't begin on the battlefield.

The military counsel:
Jesus, who is the Army General of heaven gives us the most basic military counsel in our focus.
You must first sit to count the number of soldiers in your own army and then count the number of soldiers in the army of your opponent.
the advantages and disadvantages of your own army, compared to his and then re-strategize.
Jesus went further to say; After counting, you strategize: "Can I make my own 10,000 to defeat their 20,000?" In counting, you look for strengths and weaknesses,
The coach of a team must first look into his own team, identify his key players and their fitness then consider the footballers of the other team and then strategize.
It is like a football match.
How come Christians are only told to FIGHT and FIGHT and we aren't told to first count our own army?
We don't look at our strengths and weaknesses, our

advantages and disadvantages, as well as that of the opposing soldiers. We aren't even taught the strategy!
The following are things to have to build a formidable army:
Add to your faith virtue
to virtue add knowledge
to knowledge add self-control
to self-control add perseverance
to perseverance add godliness
to godliness add brotherly kindness

 and to brotherly kindness add love.
Our enemy is immortal and we were once under his domain and numbered as his army but at Salvation
we were converted into the LORD'S ARMY.
We will not win this battle if we still walk in the flesh, which is the old man.
Have you ever wondered why after you prayed and fasted over a particular matter, it leaves you for a while but after some days or months you are back to it?
The enemy has not given up on you and you must die daily to flesh. Your army is not yet formidable.
May the Communion of the Holy Spirit be with us all... Amen.

CHAPTER 7

The Battle: The Confusion

Passage: 1 Samuel 7:7-11

Focus: 1 Samuel 7:10

"And as Samuel was offering up the burnt offering, the philistines drew near to battle against Israel: but the Lord thundered on that day upon the Philistines and discomfited them and they were smitten before Israel."

A battle is better won when the other party is in confusion. I have been to several prayer meetings and the only prayer said in the meeting were prayers against the enemy. I have met with several pastors whose area of ministerial calling is to be an enemy fighter. But the question we should ask ourselves is, "Are we doing it biblically?"

This sect are always confused whenever they read the word of Jesus concerning how we deal with the enemy. The question that we ask is "Why do we pray against our enemies when Jesus said we should love them and pray for them?" And the answer is this: People approach Christian warfare as a Mortal Combat (physical) but it should be dealt with immortally (i.e spiritually).

When we confuse the physical with the spiritual, it becomes a problem. I am aware that some human beings are wicked, their source of wickedness however is spiritual and not physical. When you face the source, you will discover that the person you thought to be wicked is just a vessel used by the devil to oppress you.. I command that demon to pack off right now, in Jesus' Name.

May the Communion of the Holy Spirit be with you! Amen

I bring the fight to the devil over this matter (mention yours). Devil, I stand against the progress of your works. [7/20, 12:38 PM] Freeman: The confusion I mean here is when the opponent don't know what to do, And a battle is best won when one's opponent is in confusion.
A battle is best termed as a fight. Let's quickly go through our Bible reading.
1 Samuel 7:7-11 [NLT]

7 When the Philistine rulers heard that Israel had gathered at Mizpah, they mobilized their army and advanced. The Israelites were badly frightened when they learned that the Philistines were approaching.

8 "Don't stop pleading with the lord our God to save us from the Philistines!" they begged Samuel.

9 So Samuel took a young lamb and offered it to the lord as a whole burnt offering. He pleaded with the lord to help

Israel, and the lord answered him.

10 Just as Samuel was sacrificing the burnt offering, the Philistines arrived to attack Israel. But the lord spoke with a mighty voice of thunder from heaven that day, and the Philistines were thrown into such confusion that the Israelites defeated them.

11 The men of Israel chased them from Mizpah to a place below Beth-car, slaughtering them all along the way.

This passage really explains the meaning if confusion to my best choice
What really got me was the fact that Samuel made a sacrifice
And this made me to understand the fact that
To God
If we truly want our enemies to be confused we must please God
One of the ways we pleases God is by our sacrifice of worship Presenting our body as a living sacrifice is another point
Sacrifice of prayer
 Living a consecrated life. Living Holy.
All this make God fight our battles for us
While you relax with your chilled soft drink and pie.
The sacrifice of becoming a Representative of light in everywhere we find ourselves
And so on.... They are more than what we even think So as Samuel sacrifice this young lamb... What happens to the

philistines was confusion

The Lord is causing confusion in the camp of our reckless enemies in Jesus name amen

Hallelujah.

Anchor verse of the scripture

1 Samuel 7:10

"And as Samuel was offering up the burnt offering, the philistines drew near to battle against Israel: but the Lord thundered on that day upon the Philistines and discomfited them and they were smitten before Israel"

I have met with several pastors whose area of ministerial calling is to be an enemy fighter.

I have been to several prayer meetings and the only prayer said in the meeting were prayers against the enemy. As I said earlier a battle is better won when the other party is in confusion.

This sect are always confused whenever they read the word of Jesus concerning how we deal with the enemy.

But the question we should ask ourselves is, "Are we doing it biblically?"

The question that we ask is "Why do we pray against our enemies when Jesus said we should love them and pray for them?"

And the answer is this: People approach Christian warfare as a Mortal Combat (physical) but it should be dealt with immortally (i.e.spiritually).

When we confuse the physical with the spiritual, it becomes a problem.

I am aware that some human beings are wicked, their

source of wickedness however is spiritual and not physical. Change your pattern of prayer today and let love rule your heart towards the supposed enemy but unmask the true enemy.

Mention the name of that person who is always against you and say in prayer that Mr. or Mrs. This or That (put the name) you're not my enemy, my enemy is the devil and I am not confused.

When you face the source, you will discover that the person you thought to be wicked is just a vessel used by the devil to oppress you.

I bring the fight to the devil over this matter (mention yours). Devil, I stand against the progress of your works.

Use this format

Brethren

Mention the matter you want to bring to fight to the devil

I command that demon to pack off right now, in Jesus' Name.

May the Communion of the Holy Spirit be with us all.. Amen.

Father I thank you for another time in your presence

I ask that you will never cease to fight for us.... In Jesus mighty name I pray amen

ACKNOWLEDGEMENT

I sincerely Acknowledge the dedication and timely commitment of all those who in one way to another made this work a success

ABOUT THE AUTHOR

Innocent Franklin

Pastor Innocent Franklin. O. hails from Umunakwa Amorka in Ihiala Local Government Anambra State.
He holds Diploma in Theology. He is married to Mrs Miracle Innocent and blessed with two children Success and Marvelous.